PROMISING FOREVER

A Falling for a Rose Wedding Edition

STEPHANIE NICOLE NORRIS

Promising Forever
A Falling for a Rose wedding special
Copyright 2019 Stephanie Nicole Norris
Love is a Drug, Ink.

To my reading family, thank you so much for your continued support!
Your love for these stories is what makes them happen time and time again.
I love you.

Chapter One

THREE DAYS BEFORE THE WEDDING

*T*he buzz of Phoebe's cell phone pulled her face from the feathered pillows she stuffed her head in, carrying a sleepy gaze to the glow that initiated a moment after. Her hand shot over, fumbling with the device in her fingers then pulling it to her now-squinting lids as she took a glance at the number.

A sigh escaped her lips, and her head plopped back into the pillow as her mind and body immediately became mobilized.

Don't answer it.

Phoebe's feet kicked underneath the sheets, her mind betraying itself while continuing to dish out instructions.

Stay strong, you can do this.

On the fifth and what Phoebe knew was the final ring, she tapped the screen and pulled the receiver to her ear.

"I hope this is an emergency," she cooed, a grin lifting her mouth as she bit down on her plump bottom lip.

"Every moment I miss without you is detrimental, my love."

Phoebe's heart raced as a shield of heat combed her skin. Hearing the baritone vocals of her fiancé Quentin Davidson made her want to throw in the towel of this absurd idea she and her triplet sisters had come up with.

Four days earlier, while they were all celebrating their upcoming trio wedding, they'd spontaneously decided to take the "keep your eyes off the bride" tradition—that was usually done *only* the day before the wedding—to the extreme. And instead, they'd agreed to go the remaining seven days without the presence of their fiancés. It was an attempt to make them all that much hungrier for each other on their wedding day, and it was a good idea that slowly but surely backfired. Four days into this madness, Phoebe, Eden, and especially Jasmine were having withdrawals, the love they were now accustomed to getting outside of their reach.

But being the one with the soundest mind and judgment, Phoebe internally reached for her resolve, reining in her sexual frustration and overloading heart.

"I miss you, too."

"Then let's put an end to this and stick with the normal tradition, babe. I can't go three more days without you."

Phoebe's heart fluttered. "Do you know how hard you're making this for me?" she whispered.

"Not as hard as my—"

"No, please, don't..." she begged before Quentin could finish his sentence.

Quentin sighed, his heavy exhale exhibiting his own frustration through the line.

"I promise it will be worth it in the end," Phoebe pushed while fighting with the tingling between her thighs.

There was a long distance silence on the other end, then, "As you wish."

Phoebe bit down on her lip again.

"I love you," his deep voice murmured.

"I love you, too."

Phoebe ended the call, then swatted her forehead with the face of the phone. If this was such a good idea, why did it feel so wrong?

She shook her head, then glanced at the time. Midnight.

"Ugh."

Phoebe stuffed her face back in the pillow, drowning out her backtracking thoughts before she reneged on her own order and returned his call.

ACROSS TOWN, JASMINE ALEXANDRIA ROSE TUMBLED OFF the bed in a hard crash onto the floor as she fought to work the vibrator clamped between her fingers.

"Shit," she cursed, tossing the stimulator across the room where it hit the wall, then fell to the plush carpet in a soft thud. "Simple ass batteries," she fumed, making no attempt to pull her unsatisfied naked body from the floor.

Staring at the ceiling, Jasmine thought about whose idea it was to keep up this charade. Sure, she, Phoebe, and Eden had all agreed, but who initially threw the idea into the air? That's whose ass she wanted to kick.

"I have never felt so uncomfortable in my life," she mumbled, exposed to the thirst she craved for her fiancé, and mayor of Chicago, Luke Steele. "What the hell, Jasmine, you're supposed to be a boss," she scolded to herself. "Surely you can handle three more days. Just three," she reassured herself, her voice trembling with uncertainty.

Her eyes crept across the light gray walls to the clock that rested against the barrier. Twelve-fifteen.

"Be like Eden and speak positive affirmations," she suggested. "You can do this, Jasmine; you've never met a challenge you were unable to face head-on. As a matter of fact, you've been through worse ordeals, right?"

The quietness around Jasmine teased her, and she shut her eyes, her hands roaming down her bare belly into the short curls of hair that rested against the mons of her sex.

The shrill of the phone cut through the silence, and yanking her hand from between her legs, Jasmine sat up straight, then folded her legs underneath her bottom as she pulled up on her knees. She stared at the bright glow from her phone resting on the bed, answering without hesitating.

"Hey, bae."

"Tell me everything's okay," his deep voice stroked.

Jasmine fell back on her butt, crushing her feet with the ampleness of her bottom.

"Yes. Everything is okay."

"I miss you."

Jasmine dropped her head, a smile lifting her lips. "I miss you more."

"Don't try me."

A tinkling laugh escaped her lips. "How would you know unless you were me?"

"Because when you know, you know. Nothing could supersede the love I have for you, not even your love for me, and I'm okay with that."

"I'm inclined to—"

"You'll never convince me otherwise, princess." The call went silent, and then he spoke again. "Are you in bed?"

Jasmine glanced down at herself on the floor. "Not quite. I mean...no, I'm not. Why do you ask?"

"I feel like breaking some rules tonight, princess. Was wondering if you felt the same."

She was hit with an instant flash of their lovemaking, extensive thick grinds from his dick tunneling her pussy. "Oh..." A moan left her mouth.

"I'll take that as a yes."

"Wait..."

On the other end of the phone, Luke sat in the driver seat of his Mercedes-Benz, outside their home in Coconut Grove.

"We have three days left, babe. We can do this."

Luke blew out a breath. "I'm not sure I agree."

Jasmine smiled, and she pulled herself on to the bed where she dropped to her back, arms spread with the phone clutched between her neck and ear. Her hands roamed over her navel.

"We could have phone sex since we've already broken the rule of communication, I suppose." The purr in her voice was laced with desire.

A growl trekked through the phone. "Princess, I am downstairs in the driveway. If I pull this dick out, I'm coming for you…"

Jasmine's body filled to the rim with heat, her nipples instantly hard and her pussy a vibrant rouse of vitality.

"Babe, you know I can't say no to you."

"Then don't."

"This is supposed to be for the betterment of our wedding night sexcapade."

"Oh…I get it, you'd rather me turn into a caveman then handle you with precision, duly noted."

Jasmine shut her eyes, bit down on her jaw, and squeezed her thighs tight.

Another sigh rippled through the phone. "I love you," he confessed.

"I love you, too."

"Get some rest tonight. I'll see you first thing in the morning."

"Luke!"

A deep chuckle came through the line. "All right, all right. I'm just messing with you."

"Good night," she murmured.

"Good night, love."

Jasmine ended the call and rolled her face into the mattress, a scream stuffed into the pillows as frustration rolled off her.

———

SIX MILES DOWN THE ROAD, EDEN ALEXANDRIA ROSE CLOSED the robe on her shoulders, tousling her hair then sweeping the strands to one side of her neck. A deep breath escaped her lips as she stared at the image reflecting off the floor-to-ceiling mirror.

"Why are you awake?" she spoke as if expecting a sure answer. Eden's gaze traveled to the clock on the nightstand in the room that was now half-empty except for the queen-sized Temper-Pedic mattress and box spring.

"Oh, that's simple, Eden, it's because you can't sleep." She paused. "And why can't you sleep, Eden?" she continued, making a show of talking to her image. "Because you've barely been engaged all of five freakin' days, and somehow, you managed to talk yourself into abstaining from your fiancé."

Eden snapped her fingers. "Tada, you played yourself." Her face fell flat just as she took a step back, her arms outstretched as her body fell backward onto the bed.

"Look at it this way," she murmured, staring at the clear acrylic ceiling fan, "you've only got three days left."

Her body twitched suddenly, as if responding to the irrationality of her proclamation.

"You can do it. You don't have a choice."

Becoming aggravated, Eden pushed off the bed, her feet slipping into a pair of house slippers as she tightened her robe and headed out of the room. She needed to take a walk, clear her mind, or drink something laced with alcohol. Maybe then she could fall asleep in a drunken stupor and rest for three straight days.

Nodding, Eden entered the kitchen and searched the cabinets only to find them just as bare as her body that was clad in a lacy negligée and covered with a thin robe.

"We should've waited before moving everything out. Now what am I supposed to do..."

What was once the humble abode for the sisters was now an echo of what used to be. After they'd all gotten engaged, one behind the other, the sisters had come to grips with the fact that it was time to move out. It was a surreal moment since the triplets shared everything, except for their men.

Being the last to get engaged—and lose her virginity, Eden felt as if the world was moving a million miles a second. While her sisters Phoebe and Jasmine had been engaged for a year, Eden's recent proposal was one week ago, and the desire to be in Derek James Clark's arms again was so undeniably daunting that Eden felt like she would drown in want.

"I need something to drink," she whispered, just as a lightbulb went off in her head. There was a store on the first floor of their luxury condominium, and it was open twenty-four hours. A smile tugged at Eden's lips as she headed for the door, her momentum building and arm tugging at the knob to open it.

As it came ajar, her footsteps halted, and her eyes enlarged.

"Derek!" she shouted, staring at her blindfolded fiancé. Her eyes combed over his smooth kissable lips, sculpted jaw, and solid musculature frame that was packed in a sharp tuxedo—black on red—that brought the vibrancy of his rich melanin skin alive.

She shut her eyes instantly and shouted, "What are you doing here? We're not supposed to see each other!"

"Come here." Derek reached for her arms, always knowing her position from the intimacy of their shared bond. He twirled Eden around, then lifted his arms to apply a blindfold over her face. After tying the silk fabric to her head, he stepped across the threshold with her in his embrace—their bodies moving in sync. "We still don't see each other..." his deep voice strummed, eliciting a flurry of tingles down her spine.

"Derek..."

She turned to him, their mouths blending as their arms clamped around each other. Heat erupted from their lips as they sucked, smacked, and slurped the taste of their tongues.

A sudden quake ruffled their core, and as Derek swallowed her mouth, his hand explored, untying Eden's robe and getting the full spectrum of her backside in his grip. His fingers tightened against her derriere, her soft body grazing against the solid shield of his own.

Derek swept Eden off her feet, carrying her with only the memory of the condo's layout to guide him into her bedroom.

With her arms around his neck, Eden withdrew from his mouth.

"Derek," she panted. "We...we..."

"I know," he said, laying her down on the bed as his lips pressed against Eden's shoulder. "We've got three days."

A shudder tremored through her, and her head fell languidly in defeat.

"But, but..."

Derek's kisses paused on Eden's neck, and he maneuvered her to face him, even though neither of them could eye each other properly.

"Do you really want me to leave?" his deep voice murmured.

Eden's heart teetered, the drum of his voice dropping a heated collation over her skin. She reached in the direction of his voice, with fingers that trailed over his succulent lips and trimmed goatee.

Derek took her fingers into his mouth and sucked Eden's digit, his tongue a stimulating brush of warmth.

"No," she whispered, "I don't want you to go."

Derek kissed down Eden's hand as he swept a palm over her thighs where he slipped into her panties and sent a pressing finger into the wet bud of her clitoris.

"Oooh..." Eden purred, her body lifting as it was struck with instant want.

"I want to show you just how much I miss you, Mona Lisa..."

Eden opened up to him, gripping his tie, where she rushed to remove it along with the button-down shirt he wore.

"Mmmm..." Her hands moved over his chiseled chest, and Derek's mouth kissed around her soft breasts, his tongue teasing her areola while he removed his suspenders and freed himself of the black slacks.

"Where is he?" Eden said, reaching for his dick, her hands grasping at air as Derek smiled.

He kissed along her mouth, then sank between Eden's legs, "Right here," Derek murmured, his cock entering her sweet heat in an elongated drill.

"Ooooh!"

Eden's nervous system jumped all at once, and every inch of her body rejoiced as Derek buried himself while kissing between her breasts.

"Ooooh... baby," Eden panted, lifting her hips to meet his rocking strokes, pound for pound with her legs locked around his waist. "Aaaah... Ooooh, my God."

Derek inhaled her nipples, pushing both breasts together as he dug and rocked, thrust after thrust, revving an ignition of heated chills that raced over their bodies, only to rise again.

"Oh, baby, I'm coming fast," Eden squealed, her body shaking as a tremor beat down her spine.

Derek traced her skin with his tongue, down her neck, up the curve of her chin to parted lips.

He clasped his hands to her thighs, lifting them over his shoulders where he drew back and forth, fucking her hard, as squirts of her passion drowned his shaft.

"Ooooh, Derek!" she screamed just as he murmured, "Mona Lisa..." His jaw locking, his pounding exploding in a whip of feverish hammering.

Screams drifted into the one o'clock hour, and as they satisfied their need for one another, neither Eden nor Derek gave a second thought about the time.

Chapter Two

"*Y*ou did what?!" Phoebe and Jasmine yelled, their eyes wide as they stared over at their identical sister.

"It was a mistake," Eden blushed, her leg bouncing as it rested over the other.

"Ah hell nawl, I'm calling Luke." Jasmine turned and shoved her hand to the bottom of her purse, her fingers fishing for the smartphone she'd dropped inside when they arrived. Seated inside Jerrod's Italian restaurant for lunch, the sisters were there to go over a last-minute checklist when Eden let it slip that she'd slept with Derek.

"No! Jasmine."

Phoebe reached to grab her sister's hand, making Jasmine struggle as she tried to dial her fiancé.

"Let me go, Phoebe," Jasmine said.

"No!"

They arm-wrestled for the phone.

"Jasmine!"

"Maaaaaan, I've gone four days straight without my boo, and you know we have an active sex life, but the Virgin Mary is getting more dick than me, no."

Jasmine continued to wrestle for the phone, but Phoebe fought back, determined to get through to her sister.

"Listen to me!" Phoebe shouted, making Jasmine go still, her nostrils flaring as she stared at Phoebe.

"We can do this."

"Who is we? Because the plans are screwed now that Mona Lisa been getting her freak on."

Eden squinted her eyes at Jasmine and pursed her lips as a giggle slipped from Phoebe's mouth. Jasmine scowled right back at her sister, tilting her head as if to say *and what?*

"Don't you dare call me that. Sounds scandalized when you say it."

Phoebe's laugh brought the glare of Jasmine's scowl to her.

"Listen, this isn't helping either of us," Phoebe said. She eyed Jasmine. "Can you put your phone away, please? We will forgive our sister and continue to get through this together. We've had harder obstacles in our life before, right?"

"When?" Jasmine challenged.

"Last year, when we were arrested for stealing my

wedding dress."

"We didn't steal your wedding dress. You were being fitted at the bridal boutique when Samiyah went into labor, and we rushed her to the hospital. None of us was thinking about the dress you had on."

"This is true, but it was still an obstacle. You were busy building protestors to march down on the precinct. Meanwhile, Eden and I were stuck dealing with Blaire."

Jasmine's nose scrunched. "Who's Blaire?"

Eden shuddered. "The sex worker who we were behind bars with," she mumbled as the memory of Blaire demonstrating a body search resurfaced.

Dressed in a miniskirt, see-through body-hugging top, six-inch heels, and 1980s-styled hair with heavy makeup, Blaire introduced herself and proceeded to demonstrate a search.

"If you have any contraband, like say, a lighter," she pressed, *"the guard will make you squat, like this."* Blair squatted with her feet apart. *"Then he'll make you cough, so if you do have something, it'll fall out. Now if you've got strong pussy muscles like me, then it doesn't matter what they do. They can ask you to take a shit, you're still going to hold that lighter clamped against those walls, you know."* Blaire shook her head. *"They think they can get anything to drop out that way, and don't get me wrong, they can with most, but I smuggle shit in every time."* Blaire cleared her throat. *"Just last week when they caught me with my trick on 38th and Fairmount, I stuck a roll of quarters in my pussy."* Blaire shrugged. *"I'd just gotten*

paid and the john only had change wrapped in that damn bank paper. They never found it, either. Hell, I've hidden dicks the size of Alaska in this poo-tang, forget about a roll of quarters."

Eden and Phoebe shuddered at the memory, while Jasmine held a brow quirked, her lips twisted.

"That does sound pretty bad," Jasmine said. "Still, it only lasted what, a few hours?"

"The most uncomfortable hours of my life," Eden added.

Jasmine peered at her. "Yeah, now join the party. Oh I forgot, you can't because you've broken the rules and got your freak on when you were probably the one that came up with this idea anyway."

"Come on now, Jasmine, don't start pointing fingers because you're frustrated," Phoebe quipped.

"Then it must have been you," Jasmine reiterated, "how else could you be so calm about it?"

Phoebe opened her mouth to respond, her brows dipping as a scowl stretched across her face. "I wasn't—"

"We should be talking about what we're going to do about our wedding dress problem. Not something we can do nothing about."

"Oh, you would like that, wouldn't you," Jasmine said, rolling her eyes as she sat back against her chair and crossed her legs—her foot bouncing from her antsy upsurge of emotions.

Eden sighed harshly. "Okay, I messed up. It isn't as if I went looking for him. I opened the door, and he was there!" she mumbled. "Sexy as all hell, and I tried to turn him away."

"Mmm-hmm, sure you did," Jasmine murmured.

"Eden is right, Jasmine."

Jasmine rolled her eyes at Phoebe and mumbled again.

"I'm with you," Phoebe reassured Jasmine. "Quentin called me last night, too and...whew." Phoebe shook off a shiver.

"But you held strong, as did I even after almost breaking my neck," Jasmine said with an upturn of her eyes.

Eden and Phoebe pursed their lips in question when Jasmine explained in a low murmur. "I was trying to get the thingy to work, my batteries ran out." She tossed her hands up. "Whatever. Let's talk about the dresses before I get angry all over again."

"Oh, so you're not angry now, then?"

Jasmine's eyes fell to a squint as her glare shot daggers over at Eden.

"I could keep going. I do have more to say."

Phoebe held her arms out, her hands up to put an end to the back-and-forth between her sisters. "No, please, let's not."

"Freak," Jasmine mumbled as she kept her eyes on Eden.

Eden gasped and a laugh shot from Phoebe's lips.

"You did not just call me a freak!"

Phoebe's laughter consumed them all, and before long, all three of them were chuckling at the thought.

"Got your first piece of dick, and now you've lost your mind."

"And if this is losing it, I never want to find it again."

The women laughed harder as curious stares from neighboring customers glanced their way.

A round of flashes went off, and Eden chimed, "We're going to be in tomorrow's news."

"By now you should be accustomed to having your picture taken," Jasmine said.

"Not here. This is the spot where we're supposed to be safe," Eden responded.

"Yeah, well, even after having an understanding with the owner, a few will still get a picture in here and there; it's normal at this point."

"What about Cadence and Cadena?" Eden asked in reference to the royal twins from the African tribe Kéra Asnela who were in Chicago specifically for the triplet wedding.

Since partnering with the royal family in an effort to bring a pipeline of resources, including vegetation, to alleviate the hunger crisis in the city of Chicago, King Isaac Winthrope and his royal family—including Princesses Cadence and Cadena—were invited to the wedding. The invitations were promptly accepted, and the Royals were expected to all attend.

"We picked this spot because we hoped they would be

safe from prying eyes. If they're not, should we leave and reschedule this lunch?"

Phoebe waved her hand. "No, no. I'm sure the princesses are more accustomed to being in the spotlight than we are."

"Speaking of princesses," Jasmine added as all eyes turned to the incessant flashing of cameras that now seemed to go on for a lifetime.

"I think it's safe to say we've been fooling ourselves to ever think we'd be safe at any public building with these two."

Phoebe and Eden nodded as they observed the twins, confidence oozing from them as they sauntered with catwalk strolls across the room. Surrounding them, men in royal attire, with stern faces and eyes ever observant, were no doubt their royal guards.

As they progressed closer, a different set of men dressed in austere black suits and secret service-type earpieces moved to cover the triplets as their own security were also a force to be reckoned with.

When the twins paused in front of their table, everyone held their positions. No more than sixty seconds later, the restaurant was emptied but not without a fuss as some patrons were not through dining.

Promises for free meals were handed out as the owner, and his employees escorted customers out of the door, with some patrons threatening to leave a vile review on the business' website.

With the venue now silent and the two sets of identical sisters focused on one another, both security teams departed, aligning themselves around the restaurant as Cadence and Cadena were offered chairs. They sat with self-assurance, poised and legs crossed. The vibrancy of their melanin skin was enhanced by the canary yellow jackets that hid their necks with tall collars, shielding their arms with dolman sleeves, black suit pants, and canary yellow spiked heels. The triplets eyed the twins carefully, appreciating the fashion of their fascinator hats that sat at an angle, round and flat at the front of their head.

"Good afternoon," they all chimed, a chuckle skipping throughout them as they spoke in unison.

"Thank you for meeting my sisters and me here," Phoebe said. "It was brought to our attention that you could possibly help with our bridal gown quandary."

"Yes," Cadence spoke up, a wide smile spreading her lips. "Our team of seamstresses can have a custom gown presented to you within seventy-two hours. We would need your measurements which we can access if you'll follow us back to our estate. However, it will have to be done today."

Cadena lifted her arm and glanced at her watch. "Now would be preferable." Cadena's tone was no-nonsense, her facial expression stoic, her posture proper and unmoving.

It was clear that Cadence was the eccentric one of the two.

"How are the accommodations of your home; are you

pleased?" Phoebe asked.

The twins smiled, which was a rare occurrence for Cadena. A gleam twinkled through Cadence's gaze.

"Your brother Jacob is one of a kind. His architectural skills are on a level of their own. We are pleased with our state palace, and it would be our pleasure to have you over so we can honor your sacred day with the gift of custom gowns."

"A gift?"

"Of course," Cadena drawled. "Surely, you didn't think we would ask for compensation?"

"That's usually how it works," Jasmine spoke up.

Cadena turned her low-lidded sharp gaze on Jasmine, a faint smile surfacing on her lips as Jasmine's smart retort settled in her spirit.

"That will never be the case when you're dealing with the Royals of Kéra Asnela," Cadena assured.

Jasmine and Cadena held their eyes on one another, an understanding of strongminded wills correlating between them.

"In that case, we would love to accept your generous gift," Eden said. She glanced between Phoebe and Jasmine. "Right, ladies?"

"We would," Phoebe and Jasmine chimed.

"Gemini," Cadena called.

The biggest man of the royal guard, six feet five inches in height and exuding iron-clad bravado, approached the table within seconds.

He gave a short head bow. "Your Highness," his deep voice thundered.

Without giving him eye contact, Cadena addressed Gemini as she wrestled with an uncanny elixir of heat that cloaked her skin.

"We're leaving. Escort our guests back to the estate please."

Gemini hesitated, prompting Cadena to lift an eye and meet his heavy gaze.

A whistle slipped from Gemini's lips, and he pulled his eye from Cadena's cinnamon face as his right-hand man approached.

"Jasir, escort our guests back to the royal estate."

"No," Cadena asserted.

Gemini's heavy gaze drifted back to Cadena.

"I asked *you* to escort our guests. Jasir will escort Cadence and I."

"Your Highness, it is my duty to protect you at all times by order of the King."

"You are also to follow my orders when outside of the King's presence." Cadena glanced around to make a show of looking for King Isaac Winthrope. "I don't see my father, so should I asked again or will following my lead be a problem for you?"

They eyed each other, long and hard, a battle of wills that shifted the atmosphere around them.

Watching with keen interest Phoebe, Eden, and

Jasmine glanced between Cadena and Gemini, their obvious fight more than what the eye could see.

"As you wish, Your Highness."

"Thank you."

"If I may cut in," Phoebe added, "We have our own security. There's no need for any of your men to escort us."

Jasmine and Eden agreed with a head nod.

"Besides, this is our city, we kinda own the joint," Jasmine added.

Eden chuckled as Phoebe glanced at Jasmine with a broad smile, eyes enlarged. "We kinda own the joint? You've been around Carla too long," she said in reference to their close friend Carla Jones.

Jasmine winked. "You might be right about that."

"Are you sure?" Gemini asked.

"We are certain."

The triplets rose to their feet, and on cue, their security surrounded them, in line to escort the three wherever they were going next.

When Cadena moved to stand, Gemini slipped behind her seat, adjusting her chair as she rose.

"Where would you like to have me now, Your Highness?"

The dark thread of his voice rippled down Cadena's spine. She knew where she wanted him, but nothing about those inhibitions were like her, and somehow she had to rid herself of the sudden lust in her spirit, even if that meant removing Gemini from her detail altogether.

Chapter Three

"Awww, man, you've got to be kidding me!"

Derek James Clark slipped his hands inside the black slacks of his Ferragamo suit pants, a smile lifting his mouth as he eyed his brethren with amusing sorrow.

"I had to," Derek said. "I don't see how either of you can stand it."

Quentin lifted the bar onto the bench and sat up, sweat dripping down his forehead from the intense workout.

As the multimillionaire business tycoon of thirty-two fitness centers scattered throughout the southeast and southwest regions, Quentin's daily regimen was consistently packed with sustaining his muscle tone and healthy lifestyle. Today, however, his routine was the most rigorous weightlifting he'd done in a while, mainly due to the frustration of being without his fiancée Phoebe Alexandria Rose.

"I knew I should've gone up there while she was on the phone purring at me in that sexy-ass voice that always gets my dick hard." He sighed.

Luke slapped Quentin on the shoulder, "Phone sex," he murmured, "it was the option I was given."

"That's your problem," Derek said. "I wasn't given an option. I took it."

The men groaned again. "And you decided to come here and gloat about it," Quentin said. "In a suit, no less."

"I could use a good workout, and you know I keep a bag in the locker in the back."

"No, I don't know. I haven't seen you since the engagement dinner last week."

"Plans, my brother."

"What are these plans, exactly?"

Derek chuckled, aware of the change of conversation that was happening.

"You know Eden's taking the position to headline the design firm in Bali, and I've just purchased our first home there as a wedding gift and surprise."

Quentin's and Luke's thick brows rose.

"Nice," Luke said. "How often will you get a chance to travel back home to Chicago?"

Derek glanced over at Luke. "It's our choice, but more than likely weekends, to start." A smile hovered on his lips. "Are you all going to miss me?"

The men laughed. "Nah, in any case, we'll just jump on

a plane and come to you all. I'm sure surprise visits from her sisters would make Phoebe's day."

"More than that, we could use a trip to Bali."

"Yeah..." Derek said, "I could show you the stomping grounds."

The men chuckled. "You say that as if you grew up there."

"I've gotten a pretty good look of the lay of the land. You know my mind is like a map, once I've been somewhere once, it would take amnesia for me to forget my routes. It's what makes me the best in my field, knowing the area, its surroundings, and the things that make it stand out."

Being one of Chicago's top award-winning real-estate moguls, Derek James Clark had an eye for excellent property. Not only that, but the neighborhoods were essential to picking a place for him and Eden to live without the disturbance of the news or paparazzi across the seas. Even so, they were minutes from Tegalalang Rice Terrace and the infamous monkey forest they'd visited during their trip months earlier.

"Eden is going to love it," he said, the smile on his face broadening as he thought of her eyes lightening up, mouth agape, and heart full.

"What she's going to love more is that you're moving there with her," Luke added.

Quentin nodded. "Yeah, we were under the impression

that you would travel back and forth regularly but not actually make the move."

Derek twisted his lips. "Would you leave Phoebe if it—"

"Nah," Quentin cut him off. "Nothing could keep me away from her... except this insane agreement she made that prohibits us from being together until the wedding."

Derek chuckled while Luke pulled in his bottom lip with his teeth.

"I think you find our agony too amusing, my brother," Luke said.

Derek nodded. "I do, and I don't."

"It can't be both," Luke continued.

"Not usually. I get it, an oxymoron and all that jazz; however, I know what that's like, I was there, but—" Derek sucked off his teeth, "—take charge, fellas."

He chuckled as he strolled away, headed to the locker room to change and get his regular workout in.

Glancing at each other, Quentin and Luke exhaled harshly, both making up their mind to break up this back-and-forth song and dance.

———

Two Days before the Wedding

"If I didn't know any better, I would swear you were trying to keep your eye on me." Jasmine folded her arms and glanced at Phoebe, unamused by the escort her sister had become whenever Jasmine needed to go out.

"What are you talking about? We're shopping. This is what we do."

"Mmm-hmm, we've never gone shopping in a convenience store, nor whenever I have to use the ladies' room. Just admit it, you're trying to watch me in case I decide to go after Luke."

Phoebe grabbed a bag of Lay's potato chips, then lifted them high and shook them in front of Jasmine. "See, you're being paranoid. I came in here because I wanted a snack."

"Phoebe, you don't eat potato chips." Jasmine snatched the bag out of Phoebe's hand. "Do you think I'm going to climb out of the back window or something? I'm trying to figure out your obsession with me right now. You know our security won't fit through that small hole, right?"

Phoebe sighed, her truth uncovered.

"I don't see you sitting in the car looking after Eden, and Ms. Buss-Me-Down is the one you should be watching."

Phoebe cracked a smile. "What's up with you and your metaphors with Eden? You're sounding more and more like Carla, should I be worried?"

"Maybe when I'm not so sexually frustrated, I can get back to my normal self."

"I've got just the thing to take your mind off of your woes."

"Oh really, because I've tried four different vibrators, and nothing is doing the trick."

Phoebe gasped. "Are you serious right now?"

Jasmine eyed her sister with a squint. "I think you know the answer to that."

Phoebe pressed her lips together and held back a laugh.

"It ain't funny either, now tell me what it is that you have that can take my mind off of this besides my soon-to-be husband's—"

"Okay, okay!"

"I'm just saying."

"I got your saying, please believe it." Phoebe paused. "I was thinking. Once upon a time, Quentin and I were talking about how awesome it would be to find out our heritage. I remember a conversation between you, me, and Eden about the same thing when we were kids, remember?"

Jasmine twisted her lips. "You can't be talking about when we were playing around with the idea of having lineage from a grandiose African tribe, right?"

"I am. And since this could very well be our last time together like this, now is as good a time as any to get our ancestry checked."

"You're talking about a DNA test?"

"Yeah, I know a place that I've been eyeing for a while.

We should go and possibly surprise the fellas with our results."

A smile pushed Jasmine's lips up her face.

"Eden is leaving for Bali, we're all moving out and moving on with our lives, this could be our last great venture together for a while or who knows... forever, maybe."

"Okay, hold on for a minute there, don't go so far," Jasmine said, uncomfortable with the thought of being away from her sisters "forever." The trio had been as thick as thieves their entire childhood and adult lives.

"This is really happening, isn't it?" Jasmine's voice grew somber as she stared at the soft reflection to her spunkiness straight ahead.

"Yeah." Phoebe's voice dropped to a soft, mellow tone, and both of their hearts palpitated with an earnest happiness that weighed them down. Without another word, the two tossed their arms around each other in a tight hug that crashed their hearts yet kept their spirits lifted.

The doorbell to the convenience store chimed, and Eden blurted, "What is this? Hugs without me?"

Jasmine and Phoebe laughed as they opened up, receiving Eden as she flew into their arms, the three locking tightly around each other, their embraces as strong as the love they carried for one another.

"I love you both," Jasmine said, their foreheads pressed together.

"We love you, too," Eden and Phoebe chimed.

"How about that ancestry test, yes?"

Eden gasped. "Really?"

Jasmine and Phoebe laughed with a nod.

"Let's go!"

Chapter Four

The swing of the front door was met with a soft click as Jasmine crossed the threshold, closing it behind her. She sighed. Today had been somewhat eventful. As much as she missed Luke, being with her sisters, commemorating their upbringing and where they were in life presently fulfilled her in more ways than one.

Being the star of a daytime soap opera, a political activist, and one-third of a famous set of triplets kept Jasmine busy. Reflecting on the bond shared with her sisters, brothers, and the relationship she cherished with her father and mentor Christopher Lee Rose came second to nothing else. But Jasmine had never felt guilty about officially moving on until the realization hit her today that she and her sisters were departing, officially set to marry the men of their dreams and possibly having their lives change so drastically that she'd miss them something terrible.

Jasmine swallowed a knot in her throat, her mind wandering to her late mother Janet, who'd passed away from a home invasion when she and her sisters were infants. Never having the chance to meet her mother with the knowledge of who she was, her hopes, dreams, what she wanted to accomplish in life, covered Jasmine's heart in melancholy more often than she cared to admit. However, she was grateful for the support of her family, and she planned to make it her business to assure the relationship they'd grown to love remained, even after marriage and beyond.

"Mrs. Jasmine Alexandria Steele," she murmured, her mind traveling back to Luke just as her eyes fell on a single line of rose petals just beyond the exit of the foyer.

Jasmine's mouth parted, her heart picking up eccentric speed as she hoped the petals were placed there by Luke. At the same time, she feared one of the fans from her show had broken inside in an attempt to woo her. Crazier things had happened to her co-stars, and some of the fan mail she'd received leaned toward stalker-like activity. With that thought set in her mind, her next decision was to retreat. With her hand reaching for the doorknob, the sudden anxiety shifted, altering the distress with a calmness that covered her heart and gave her the bravado to proceed forward.

Jasmine's legs moved, one foot in front of the other, as

she crept into the next room, her eyes sweeping around the interior in search of the intruder. Darkness had taken over, except for the flick of a lingering candle that had burned almost to its base sitting in one of the golden candlesticks Eden had added to the space after her initial design.

"It appears I'll have to fire your security detail," a dark voice murmured.

A soft gasp flew from Jasmine's lips, and she spun on her heels, eyes cloaked in wonder as her sight took in widespread mammoth shoulders driven into sinewy muscled flesh packed over solid washboard abs. The intake of breath damn near knocked her sideways as her eyes settled on the sharp cut of his waist, the absurdity of his dick print flexing against the fabric of gray sweatpants.

Luke moved toward her, his bare feet large enough to fill two of Jasmine's size six-and-a-half shoes.

"Baby, what are you doing here?" Her voice had transformed into a breathlessness she recognized when filled with unequivocal want.

His response came with the sweep of her body as he lifted her into his arms, keeping a stern eye trained on the intricate details that formed her face. "I came for you." His dark gaze ruffled her feathers. "And I wasn't kidding about firing your security detail."

"I sent them home."

Luke peered at her. "Why would you when they hadn't checked the interior?"

Jasmine swallowed. "I feel safe here."

His gaze softened. "Always have," she added. "You're not supposed to be here, babe." It was her attempt to say she tried, even as her pussy danced a happy beat between her thighs.

"Tell me to leave, and I'll go."

Jasmine opened her mouth to speak, her words choking and her tongue inhaled by the hungry fever of Luke's mouth as his hands sank into her flesh with a ferocious grip.

"Mmmm..." she moaned, her body entrenched with fire that sprinkled her core, and crackled a sparkling tingle amid the folds of her pussy.

He spoke against her mouth. "One word." He kissed her lips, licked up her mouth, then slid down to her chin—soft, warm nibbles that knotted her nipples and threw disorder to her plum. "Order me to go," he whispered, with soft caresses down her neck, around the edge of her ear, across the heated flesh of her shoulder that was exposed from the halter top sundress she wore.

"I can't hear you, princess," his deep voice grooved.

"I... I..."

His tongue latched onto the thumping thread of her pulse, sucking as he bared his teeth and pierced her flesh with a stinging love bite.

"Oh, fuck it."

Jasmine tossed her arms around his neck, holding on tight as she pulled, turning her body in a climb up his torso, her legs wrapping around his waist. Their mouths fused, bodies banged with collision as their mouths meshed, tongues sucked, and libidos rocked them in a jerk against the nearest wall.

The sudden movement tilted the candle stand and it fell to the floor, the fire doused from the winding current that drifted from their forcible mash.

Swiftly, Luke shoved the sweatpants off his hips, his dick springing forward, slapping the thick hill of Jasmine's mound just as his grip ripped her panties to shreds.

"Aah!" Jasmine yelped, encased with heat as Luke buried his shaft so deep her teeth chattered, and her body convulsed from the snatching of his dominant authority.

"I fucking miss you so much," he whispered against her mouth. "I never want to separate from you again." Luke bucked his hips, dipping, plunging, conjuring her orgasm with each upsurge of his ramming sex.

"Ooooh my God! Luke! Baby..."

He churned her core, rocking with a grip on her ass as he speared back and forth, his fingers burying in her flesh, his dick coated with the wet heat from her canal. Slaps ricocheted between them, skin burning as they ignited their connection in a blaze that covered their skin in chills and turned their coupling into a carnal, pounding fight that rippled a wave of thundering palpitations from the clashing of their bodies.

"Mr. Mayor..." Jasmine purred, further revving Luke's engine.

"You know it turns me on when you talk like that." He

sucked in the whole of her tongue as the ridges of his cock massaged her walls in a grooving melody that made her body hum as if their flesh created a tune only their coupling could sing.

Drowned in his love and the erotic entanglement of his greedy tongue, Jasmine's eyes rolled to the back of her head, her toes curling and nails gripping as Luke fucked her hard, relentlessly beckoning Jasmine to succumb to the needy, insidious abduction of her come.

"Ooooh my Goooood!" Jasmine wailed, her body shaken as a dam broke within her, glazing Luke's dick, her back stiff, jaw locked, and eyes closed.

Luke didn't let up, pounding, thrusting, stroking Jasmine's core in an assault that sent a crazed silly screech sailing from her lips.

"Luuuuuuuke!

"I love you, I love you, I love you," he growled, crashing into her center as he stole her mouth again and came so hard that heat burst from them in what felt like a million tiny embers.

Ears popping, bodies buzzing, cores disseminating, Luke and Jasmine melted into one another, breaths heating their faces as hurried wisps of air pounced between their mouths.

"I love you, too," Jasmine purred, her body sated and on a high like she'd just been giving the biggest dose of drugs she'd ever had in her life.

"Enough to go for round one?" he asked.

Jasmine's brow arched. "That wasn't round one?"

"Nah, that was the warm-up."

With that, Luke carried her to the bedroom where they made love until the sun rose the next morning.

The Day before the Wedding

PHOEBE REDIALED JASMINE, BUT AGAIN HER CALL HAD GONE to voicemail.

"What is she doing?" she fussed, putting the car in park and then exiting the vehicle to make her way to the front door.

Today she, Eden, and Jasmine were headed to the Winthrope palace after getting a call early this morning that their dresses were ready for them to try on. Afterward, they would head to the rehearsal dinner that would include a short wine and cheese tasting at Architectural Artifacts, the eighty-thousand square foot venue that would house the triplets, their grooms, and their guests for the wedding.

Standing at Jasmine and Luke's current residence, Phoebe rang the doorbell while redialing Jasmine once more. She turned back to the car to cut her eyes at Eden, who sat in the passenger seat with a shrug when the front door opened.

Phoebe turned to face a half-naked Jasmine who covered her bare breasts with her arms while wearing a pair of Luke's boxer shorts as her bottoms.

Phoebe squinted. "I've been calling you for hours! Why aren't you answering your phone?"

Jasmine's lashes fluttered, her eyes hazy as she appeared disoriented.

"What time is it?"

Phoebe squinted harder. "What time is it? Girl, what is going on here? Are you drunk?"

"Princess, come back to bed," a deep voice boomed from the background.

Phoebe gasped. "You didn't," she said, her face turning into a mask of disappointment.

"It wasn't my fault. I came home, and he was here, and I tried to turn him away, but—"

Phoebe sighed harshly, doing an about-face as she walked away from Jasmine's naked form.

"Phoebe!"

Jasmine tiptoed in a jog to catch up with Phoebe, thankful that their house sat on its own property surrounded by a massive brick wall and a gate that was protected by a top-notch security system.

Phoebe paused and turned with a scowl on her face. "Our dresses are ready. When you and Luke get through screwing, you can head over to the Winthrope palace and try it on yourself."

Phoebe turned to leave again, catching the widespread grin on Eden's face, her eyes balking at the sudden turn of Jasmine's situation.

"Wait! So I don't get forgiveness when you were so easy to give it to Eden?"

"You did this on purpose, Jasmine, I know you!"

Aghast, Jasmine grabbed Phoebe's arm and twirled her around.

"Look, I didn't do this on purpose! I promise, come on, Luke will tell you."

"Forget it, doesn't matter now."

"It matters if you think I willingly broke our promise. I swear I didn't!"

Phoebe eyed her sister a moment longer, the longevity of her stare daunting and making Jasmine squirm, which was rare.

Phoebe exhaled. "Just get to the palace to make sure your dress fits, okay?"

Jasmine could hear the defeat in her voice. "I will, and I'm sorry, alright?" She pleaded for understanding to which Phoebe pressed her lips together and nodded.

"I'll see you later."

Getting inside the car, Phoebe glanced at Eden who tried but failed to rein in her amusement. "Whatever," Phoebe mumbled, her mind jogging to Quentin. She missed him so much that last night she'd replayed the voicemail he left twenty-five times while she flicked her sensitive clitoris, coming with no satisfaction in sight. What was to stop her from seeing him now?

You're alone in this, but you can do it, stay strong—tomorrow's the big day.

Phoebe put the car in drive and headed to the Winthrope palace, the indecision in her spirit a constant nagging.

Chapter Five

"*O*h my God."

Running her eye over the see-through bejeweled snugly-fitting gown, Phoebe could barely contain the thrill that coursed her veins. Standing in front of the floor-to-ceiling mirror, the crystallized gown made her appear to be a walking sparkle of diamonds that trailed down an increasingly long sleeve and rode the curves of her body to her pedicured feet.

Even though she and Eden had left without Jasmine, they waited for her to arrive before all three were helped into the master designs the royal seamstresses had handmade with details that would take the average designer months to create.

How they'd pulled it off with such precision was a mystery to Phoebe, but as she glanced over at her sisters, also standing in front of their own mirrors, mouths agape, the moment had all seemed too surreal.

In a bejeweled bodice much like that of Phoebe's top half of her dress, Eden was covered in the same material. Unlike the full diamond look, Eden's diamond sleeves were cut at three-fourths of an inch, with the hem of her dress exuding a mermaid flair from her knees to its base.

Jasmine's attire was also similar, but more of a full-body crystallized pants suit. With the same jeweled bodice, short sleeves, a flaring train of solid white lace that rode over her backside to the floor. "Try this princess on for size," Jasmine murmured, reminded of Luke, and the nickname he addressed her with regularly.

They glanced between one another, smiles lifting their lips, in awe of the magnificence of the designs.

"I take it that you are satisfied, yes?"

Their eyes shifted to Princess Cadena Winthrope, all of them speechless, with only Phoebe managing to push a response from her lips.

"More than we could ever express. Are you sure you don't want compensation? I can't imagine how much this must have cost to create."

Cadena smirked. "Am I to answer that with a serious retort?" her throaty voice asked.

They stared at her a moment longer. One by one, they turned back to the image that sparkled from the mirrors before them.

"Thank you, Princess Winthrope," Eden said.

"Please, don't address me as Princess anything. I prefer 'advisor to the King,' but for now, just Cadena will do."

"Cadena, this is absolutely amazing. You have saved our lives."

"Glad I could be of service." Cadena's lidded gaze traveled to her wristwatch. "Your rehearsal dinner," she prompted, reminding the triplets that the time was drawing near.

"Oh yes," they said, but none of them moved, still awestruck by their sparkling images in the mirror.

"If there's anything else I can do for you, let me know."

"Actually, there is," Phoebe chimed.

A long brow arched on Cadena's face.

"When it's your turn to say *I do*, please send us an invitation. We'd love to return the favor of gifts, in our own American way."

Cadena's face removed all signs of expression.

"You'll be waiting a lifetime for that, but I'll make sure to inform Cadence since she's likely to find her prince before me."

Cadena's gaze skipped around the room as if expecting to be caught red-handed by a lie that she had no business speaking.

The triplets frowned. "Don't be so sure. We are aware that it's royal tradition for the princess to be married to a prince that will align family ties. Is that not the case with you?"

Cadena was silent for a moment, her thoughts traveling to Gemini before shaking them off quickly.

"I don't desire to wed the traditional way, or at all if it were up to me. However, I respect my father and trust his judgment more than my own. If he saw fit for our family to become allied with another, then I would wed the prince of his choice."

Outside the room on standby, Gemini felt an unceremonious squeeze to his heart. It was forbidden for him to garner any sentiments of love for the princess, but that didn't prevent his heart from yearning for her any less.

Still, he would keep his mind focused on his duties and force himself to remain at her side, even if watching her wed caused disruption to his soul.

Architectural Artifacts

Rehearsal Dinner

"You know it's bad luck for the bride to walk down the aisle during the rehearsal, right?"

Eden Alexandria Rose questioned Carla Jones' comment with a lift of her brow.

"You haven't heard that before?"

"No. How do you know that to be true?"

"It's a superstition," Jasmine said. "It's widely believed, apparently."

Eden clutched the pearls that hugged her neck. "Okay, so what are we going to do, there's no way I need bad luck with everything Derek and I have gone through to get to this point." Eden's long dramatic lashes fluttered, anxiety riddling her bones. "Who should we ask to take our place?" Eden turned her eyes back to Carla.

"Oh no. I love you all to pieces, but, baby, listen...the tradition is that no one in the wedding party can do this. It should be a member of the audience or something. Besides, I plan to tie the knot one day, and the last thing I need is some voodoo on my spirit because of a rehearsal dinner."

"You act as if you have a future date in mind, Carla," Eden said.

"Not a date," Carla's gaze shifted to Jacob Alexander Rose, the triplet's brother and the man she'd been courting in her mind. "But a future wedding, no doubt." She winked over at Jacob, unashamed to flirt with him in public. With his intense gaze lingering her way, his thick brow moved as he winked back.

"Besides, don't you want another sister?" she exclaimed, a smile lifting the corners of her lips.

"Oh my God," Eden turned to Jasmine. "What are we going to do?"

"Calm down, sis. Norma, Martha Jean, and Adeline are going to be our stand-in brides."

Carla snapped her fingers. "That's perfect. Norma's married to your father already so that's not something you'll have to worry about. Martha Jean...eh...well, I caught her and your uncle Antonio coming out of the bathroom a few minutes ago, but I don't think either of them cares about superstitions."

A gasp fell from Eden's lips. "What!?" Eden and Jasmine chimed simultaneously.

Carla zipped her lips with her hands, signing across her mouth.

"It's too late now," Jasmine said. "If you're going to tell it, you might as well tell it all!"

"There's really not much to tell except that it's obvious your sister-in-law's mom is fucking your uncle."

This time, both Eden and Jasmine gasped, their hands lifting to their necks in a clutch.

"Why are you so forthright and nasty?" Jasmine asked.

"Wouldn't you rather me be me, or should I just beat around the bush? Matter of fact, don't answer that because it's not in my nature to bullshit around."

Jasmine held back a smirk. Truth be told, she loved Carla's frankness; it reminded Jasmine of herself.

"I think you're wearing off on me. I gotta stop hanging around you."

Carla placed a hand across her russet blouse as if offended by Jasmine's insinuation. "Take that back."

Jasmine chuckled. "I can't, it's true. But don't worry, I love you too much to disassociate with you now."

A smile replaced the appalled look on Carla's face. "Oh well, in that case. Carry on."

The ladies laughed just as a microphone was tapped, bringing everyone's attention to the front of the room where the triplets' father, Christopher Lee Rose, stood at attention.

"Mic check, one two, one two," his baritone voice drummed.

Carla zeroed in on Jacob, who stood by his father; the same height, a similar muscle tone and build holding the deliciousness of his thick brows, and full lips. Her body reacted in stimulation as she combed an eye over his smooth chocolate skin, and wished for a second she could get lost inside the same bathroom that Martha Jean and Antonio had just come out of.

She ran a hand through her jet-black bob and crossed her legs to calm her pussy down just as a server passed the table.

"Excuse me," she said, reaching for a glass of champagne from the tray that he held.

The server handed her a flute. "I'll have one, too," Eden said, swatting Carla's hand just as Carla moved one palm over her breasts.

"Thank you," Eden said to the server who nodded and moved forward. She turned her eye to Carla. "Don't start."

"What did I do?"

Eden peered at her. "You know what I'm talking about.

If you want my brother that bad, get a room. Don't start grabbing your titties in public again."

Carla rolled her eyes. "Fine." She pulled out her smartphone.

"What are you doing?" Jasmine asked.

"Getting a room, what else?"

Jasmine chuckled, and this time, Eden rolled her eyes.

"I don't know what to do with this girl."

"Love me to death."

"Hmmm."

"Good evening, family," Christopher said into the mic. "First, I want to say thank you all for joining us tonight. This is an exceptional occasion as all three of my daughters will be wed at the same time. Talk about giving an old man a heart attack."

The group of friends and family chuckled.

"We love you, Father!" Jasmine screeched.

"And I love you all, too, baby girl. To death." His gaze traveled over to Luke, Derek, and Quentin. "Speaking of death..."

"Ooooh," the crowd mock-warning crooned, having an inkling where Father Rose was going with that sentence.

"I've had the distinct opportunity to watch you boys grow into men as you've been a part of our lives, becoming best friends with my sons since you were in junior high. That also means I know your history." He paused. "I'm willing to give you the benefit of the doubt since I've also had the opportunity to see the outstanding men you've become. However, this is the part where I threaten your lives should you so much as consider doing something not in the best interest of my daughters' hearts."

"Oh no..." Jasmine and Eden chimed.

"Where is Phoebe?" Jasmine chirped in a whisper.

Eden searched the room with her gaze. "I don't know. Haven't seen her since she said she was going to the bathroom about thirty minutes ago."

At the same time they commented on Phoebe's disappearance, Quentin rose from his seat, also searching the area for his fiancée.

"And don't come to us for help because we're on our daughter-in-law's side," Luke's father pledged.

The room erupted in laughter as the in-laws all agreed while Quentin made his exit. Down a long corridor, Quentin found a stairwell and took the case two steps at a time. On the second floor, he strolled through an open doorway that led to the balcony of the venue, his gaze searching the hall. When they landed on a soft silhouette at the end of the passage on the right, he turned, strolling to her quietly, though she was aware of his presence.

"My love, I apologize for interrupting when our agreement has been clear to remain out of sight from one another." He paused. "When I didn't see you downstairs, I became anxious and had to seek you out. Is everything okay?"

With a champagne flute in her hand, Phoebe turned to

face him, her shoulder-length hair swaying as her brown eyes met his concerned gaze.

"I hoped you would come looking for me."

There was a twinkle in her eye, and her response caused Quentin to take another audacious step forward.

"You hoped?" his dark voice drummed.

Phoebe eyed the neatly styled dreadlocks that always put her in the mind of an Egyptian head crown, dark chocolate skin, succulent lips, and the sharp cut of his masculine jawline.

His ease into her space increased the rate of her heart. They were seeing each other for the first time in six days. They'd been so close to making it to seven, but six was—by far—long enough.

"Did you know this building has a wedding suite, complete with a king-size bed, fresh linen, a master bathroom, a terrace, and—"

Quentin scooped Phoebe into his arms, dragging her curvaceous body up the iron ridges of his masculine physique, where her legs encircled his waist as did her arms around his neck.

It was an instant attack, mouths diving into one another on the thread of a hungry moan as their tongues wrestled in an undulated dance that filled them to the rim with fire.

His footfalls carried them down the hall when Phoebe whispered against his mouth, "Other way."

Quentin pivoted, going in the direction he came until

coming upon an opened double-door entry into the wedding suite. Their hearts raced with anticipation, and Quentin's needy hands held a grip on her ass before one of his palms lifted only to reconnect with her soft bouncing derriere with a stinging smack.

"Ooh..." Phoebe moaned, her pussy craving him even more than the days leading up to the moment. "Thank you," she whispered as his tongue traced the outline of her mouth.

His gaze bore into her. "For what?"

"Waiting... you did good," Phoebe reiterated. "We did good."

Quentin smirked. "There is but one day left. If you want to stick with the plans, we can part now and still make it to tomorrow."

Phoebe's brow rose. "Okay, I would like that."

Quentin tried to hide his disappointment. After all, he'd hoped she would ask him to stay, but he was willing to carry out her wishes, nonetheless. His movements slowed as he went to put her down.

"I'm just kidding," she whispered. "My hunger for you has superseded my wish to abstain. Unless you want—"

Quentin ate up her mouth again, his grip reclaiming control as her slow descent to the floor was quickly wrapped back around his body. They rid one other of their clothes after making it to the bed where he flipped Phoebe on her stomach and crawled between her legs.

His elongated dick teased her ass as he leaned over her

back, his mouth connecting with her bare shoulders in a melody of kisses. Warmth from his lips trailed down her back, sizzling her skin with each warm caressing connection of his kiss.

Phoebe trembled, her nipples stinging as they tightened with each erotic drag of his dick across her ass.

"Please," she panted, "give it to me."

Without hesitation, Quentin lifted into her pussy, expanding her sanctum in a stretching drive with the extensive stroke of his cock.

"Aaaah!" Phoebe yelped, her mouth overtaken by the strong consumption of Quentin's demanding lips.

He kept her elevated at the waist with a hand, while the other fiddled with her bobbing nipples that swayed with each thrust in and out, digging and grinding so deep his dick bent inside her, making her wail.

Her screams found no place into the atmosphere, as they were swallowed by his tongue, their passion building and bodies molding into one another.

"Mmmm," Phoebe moaned, her jutting ass bouncing and rocking, as Quentin's projectile clashes reached every inch of her core.

He wanted to express the depth of his desire for her, in marriage, in life, in sexual pleasure, but at the moment, Quentin could only bask in her love, sending that same message with each pummeling, thwarted jerk that tantalized his rock-hard dick and ignited his loins in sweltering heat.

The bed shook underneath them, and Phoebe's toes dug into the mattress, causing her ass to lift higher, giving Quentin the utmost angle to probe the wet suction of her vagina.

His mouth pulled from hers, and his hands dropped from her body as he braced them on the mattress, hoisting his hips in the position of a runner prepared for a relay race. He pounded her sex, stretching his extensive body over the back of her, and with Phoebe's head thrown in a passionate arch, he retook her mouth, the intensity of his stroke jacking so thoroughly that tears sprang from her eyes.

She couldn't hold on any longer, and when she pulled from his mouth on a scream, Quentin anticipated her plummet, gripping her neck and refusing to let her mouth go. It increased the undulating savagery of his stroke as he leaned in an angle and fucked her until her pussy squirted like the beat of a heart, with each pulsating release of her plum.

She bit down on his lip, pricking with such intensity that a drop of blood spilled from her bite. He fucked her harder, his dick now covered in crème as he ejaculated inside her, his unrelenting strokes pulling her apart and making Phoebe lose her mind.

"Aaaah! Fuccck!" they screamed simultaneously, wrapped in a layer of fire that crackled off their skin as their bodies continued to jerk from the power of their orgasms.

The tingling vibration running through their skin went on as Quentin recovered her form with his arms, crashing to the side as he cuddled her in an embrace.

They laid there together, unmoving, with bated breath as Quentin inhaled the sexual fragrance of her neck and kissed against her skin.

"I want to marry you today," he said, making Phoebe giggle.

"When you see me in my wedding dress, you'll want to marry me tomorrow."

His thoughts were invaded by an instant image of her in a beautiful white gown, sauntering toward him as the ultimate gift, his forever.

"Although our family is downstairs, I need you one more time before we part until tomorrow. I thirst for you, my love. Can you stand to let me have you once more?"

Phoebe turned in his arms, a whimper leaving her mouth from the exit of his shaft.

"Take me, I'm yours."

He did just that, filling her to the rim in a rocking grind and creating a life unbeknownst to them.

Chapter Six

THE BIG DAY

*O*f the four thousand, two hundred, and twenty-eight invitees, everyone on the guest list RSVP'd. With not an empty seat in the building, Architectural Artifacts was buzzing with an audience the size of a football stadium as guests held conversations while they waited for the ceremonies to begin.

Making rounds to assure the décor was in tip-top shape, Jada Wilson, Eden's lead designer, surveyed the main hall, delighted with the red and white colors that popped from heavy drapery and the bouquets of roses sprinkled throughout the venue. Showstopping bright red carpet ran the length of the three aisles Phoebe, Jasmine, and Eden would strut down to meet their grooms.

Jada felt as spun as a tornado each time she entered a new area—going so far as to check the silver china and red décor in the courtyard where the reception would be held.

"There you are," a deep voice brimmed.

Jada twirled to a halt, coming to face a glowing smile, deep-set dimples, and a structural jawline, laced with dark melanin skin. Her eyes popped as they ran around his goatee, up his masculine nose, into the intense intrusiveness of his gaze.

"Solomon!" Her eyes jutted around. "What are you doing here?" she crooned.

"I'm here to show support for my best friend." He stepped closer, and it was then that Jada became aware of the bouquet of purple lilies in his hand. Her heartbeat matched the sudden up-surging tempo of her pulse as Solomon offered the flowers to her.

"For me?"

"Nah, I met a random girl outside and thought she could use your favorite flowers." His smile was achingly handsome and doing crazy things to the rhythm of her heart. "Of course, they're for you, silly girl. This place is gorgeous, but I'm not surprised. Everything you touch transforms into beautiful, thriving artwork. You should let me cook your dinner afterward to celebrate."

Jada laughed nervously. Award-winning Chef Solomon McBride had been her friend since junior high school. She'd shared some of her happiest and darkest moments with him, always grateful to have his friendship. However, as of late, things between them had developed different, almost as if a shift in the atmosphere had taken place, and all she could think about was becoming more.

It ruffled her nerves so bad that at times she'd ignored his phone calls, made excuses not to visit, and put off their regular outings, pleading busy work.

Besides that, she was currently in a relationship, with an asshole who'd cheated on her more than once. Still, the lines she would cross if she were to give in to the desires of her heart could not only ruin her and Solomon's relationship but also break Marcus's heart.

Regardless of the fact that Marcus seemed fine with breaking hers, it was something Jada couldn't do. For now, she smiled and accepted Solomon's gift, along with the gentle hug of his long arms as they covered her entire back.

"Thank you," she said, the low sultriness of her voice running amok in a dance on his heart. "Let me show you to a seat, and I'll join you when the ceremony begins."

They pulled apart, and he tweaked her nose with his fingers, then slipped his large hand against hers, intertwining their fingers.

"After you."

Jada pulled him along, her nerves now scattered and her mind in overdrive as she figured out how she would make it through the night with him in the city.

IN THE GROOMS' DRESSING ROOM, QUENTIN, DEREK, AND Luke were down on their knees as the Rose men each held a hand on their shoulders, back, and midair—a spoken prayer on their lips as they lifted their friends to the Most High God. The deep density of their voices elevated as each brother blessed them with the life of their words, giving the gift of prosperity, abundance in healthy children, spiritual guidance, and longevity in love, life, and happiness.

The energy inside the bridal dressing room was much the same with Phoebe, Eden, and Jasmine holding hands while their father Christopher Lee Rose spoke a prayer in much the same manner.

But it was when the prayer had ended and Christopher presented them each with a gift that the tears the triplets attempted to hold back fell from their eyes.

Phoebe glanced from the three hair pendants back up to her father's also tearstained eyes.

"This was from Mom?" she asked, her voice clogged with tears from the weight of it all.

"It is. She purchased them all during a trip to Italy and was thoroughly excited to present them to you when you became old enough to wear them. It's taken me so long to give them to you because I didn't feel it was my place to offer them. They were her gifts to you, but I know now that the moment was meant for a time such as this."

Tears streamed down the triplets' faces, and they were immediately handed soft tissues to blot dry before messing up their foundation.

"Can you put them on us, please?" Eden's voice trembled.

"It would be my honor."

Christopher removed the pin from one silver box and stepped in front of Eden, adding the pendant to her upswept hair. It fit perfectly next to her tight bun, casting a sparkle that matched the gleam of the gown she wore.

"It's beautiful. You're beautiful," Christopher said.

Eden tossed her arms around her father and wept, with Phoebe and Jasmine joining their moment, weeping together.

Christopher attempted to take hold of the moment. "Baby girls, I love you more than life itself. I understand that today I give you away, but know I am always here for you, and you are never alone no matter what happens in your lives."

He glanced at Jasmine. "My political activist, continue to be brave and fight for injustices, be bold, and never allow anyone to mute you." He glanced at Eden. "Continue to speak positive affirmations over your life, add your husband and those closest around you and never let anyone take you for granted." He glanced to Phoebe. "Continue to be a force in the courtroom, your position in life is just an important as any, and I am proud to call you my daughter."

More tears fell from them, and Christopher positioned the pendant on Phoebe, then Jasmine. Finally, they pulled together for another warmhearted embrace.

He glanced at the clock on the wall. "It's almost time. Are you ready?"

They nodded, still blotting their makeup and trying to rein in their tears.

"I'm walking you all down the aisle one by one, so give an old man a chance to get you to your grooms."

"Dad, you're just as fit as anyone we know. Why do you act as if you're walking with a cane?"

Christopher chuckled. "You think I'm fit?" He lifted his arm and flexed a muscular bicep that pushed through his Armani suit, making the girls laugh.

There was a knock on the door. When it opened, Jada stuck her head inside.

"We're ready for you." A smile lingered on Jada's lips. "You all look beautiful." She winked over at Eden. "Gorgeous."

Eden winked back just as the ceremonial music began to play.

"Okay," Christopher held his arms up, and Phoebe, then Jasmine linked their limbs with his. "I'll be right back for you, sweetheart," he said to Eden.

Eden nodded. "I'll be waiting."

It'd taken five minutes to get Jasmine and Eden in place at the beginning of their respective aisles. Between three groups of people, they were spread far enough from each other that they would have their own walk with their father but close enough where they could catch the wink that sailed from one another along with the drops of tears that fell from their eyes as they waited for Christopher to return with Eden.

After she was in place, all three brides stared straight ahead, in awe at the magnificence of the building and the grandiose beauty Eden and Jada had managed to pull off. Phoebe was so proud of Eden; she was the ultimate workaholic who'd refused to put her duties to the side just because she was now a part of the ceremony.

"If anybody can make sure our dream wedding is fulfilled, who better than I?" she'd asked.

Jasmine and Phoebe knew what she said was true, but that didn't mean it held them off from assuring her someone else could pull it off as well. After hearing none of it, the ladies gave it a rest, and now getting the full scale of the décor in an aerial view, both ladies were glad that they had.

Just as it had been practiced the night before but with Norma in Eden's place, Eden held onto Christopher's arm as they took their first step down the aisle. The entire audience shifted to get a look at father and daughter as they moved, a crystalized shimmer sparkling from Eden's dress and the mermaid tail trailing behind as they made their way to the altar.

Eden's heart felt as if it were being handled by a drum major, palpitating so rigorously she was certain she'd break out into a sweat. This was happening, she and Derek James Clark, who'd just recently gotten engaged were getting ready to say *I do*.

"Inhale and exhale in deep breaths if you need to, sweetheart."

Eden glanced at her father as his gaze was trained on her without missing a step.

"Is it that obvious that I'm nervous?"

Christopher smiled. "Did you forget I've known you since you were in your mother's womb?"

A tear slipped from the corner of Eden's eye.

"Should we take a minute? I'm afraid if you burst into a full-fledged cry the makeup artist will fly across the room to retouch up your foundation."

Eden laughed, and they both paused their stride for a full minute so she could gather herself. She fanned her face to dry the mist of tears that clouded her vision and stared at her father, happy for his joke in the midst of her breakdown.

"Thank you."

"No thanks necessary, baby girl."

She nodded, and he took her motion as ready, then they proceeded. A deep breath fell from Eden's mouth as her gaze met Derek's, one foot off of the altar as he'd watched her progression and was headed to meet her should she need the extra assistance.

She winked his way, and through the sheer veil, he caught her gesture and winked back. A smile pulled at her lips, and in the next few steps, her arm dropped from her father's as she lifted a hand to meet Derek's and he drew her in his embrace.

Christopher's heart felt as if it would fall out of his chest. Eden's acceptance of Derek and her release from Christopher meant more to her father than she would ever know. He tried not to take it as a loss, but more of an ascension into a higher realm of love and forever. She was gone, no longer his but belonging to another man who would make decisions about her future and play a significant role in the betterment of her heart.

Tears fell from his eyes as he had his own moment of pause, watching the glow radiate from Eden's eyes as she stared up at Derek, mesmerized and fully in love.

Christopher's heart was full, and he nodded at Derek sternly, even with a tearstained face. Derek released Eden's hand and whispered to her, then took the two steps down with a hand held out, and Christopher accepted it with a manly handshake. They pulled one another in and hugged.

"You have my word that every decision I make will be in the best interest of your daughter, sir."

Christopher cleared his throat, and tears continued to stain his face as he nodded. "And you have my word, it'll be your death if you don't."

Derek guffawed and patted a firm hand on Christopher's back as the two men pulled apart.

"Touché."

Christopher nodded again, then Derek stepped back into place. Christopher turned just as a soft hand was laid on his shoulder. He glanced back, then turned full circle to Eden.

"I love you, Daddy, nothing or no one could keep me away from you too long. I promise to come bug you when we return from our honeymoon."

Christopher's burly laugh covered Eden's heart with adoration. "I look forward to it." He placed a gentle kiss on her forehead, lightly feathered as not to mess up her makeup.

Eden returned to Derek as the crowd dabbed their eyes with tissues, some hailing a full-on blow with their noses mashed into the paper as they watched Christopher make his way to Jasmine.

"Round two," Christopher murmured to himself as he held out his arm, and he and Jasmine took the same walk down the aisle.

A smile covered Jasmine's face, her stomach bubbling with excitement as she stared forward at Luke, the love of her life, her dream turned reality. His stern observation was focused as if he were counting the steps it took for her to get to him. In the same jeweled bodice, with the crystalized shimmer highlighting her melanin skin, Jasmine and Christopher watched as a few teardrops fell from Luke's awestruck gaze, making Jasmine's heart dance with each breath she took. Closing in, father and daughter paused and turned to each other, with Christopher applying a kiss to Jasmine's forehead, her eyes closing as she sucked in a deep breath.

"This is the day the Lord has made, and we will rejoice and be glad in it," he said.

Tears covered Jasmine's gaze, and she nodded.

"I love you more than life itself," Christopher added.

"I love you, too, Daddy. Please don't be sad. I don't think I can sleep well tonight knowing that you are."

The corners of his lips lifted. "Don't worry about me. I know you're in good hands. My tears are of joy, not pain or apprehension. Be great, butterfly, and soar."

He kissed her forehead again and handed her off to Luke who stepped down to meet them, claiming Jasmine's hand and shaking Christopher's simultaneously. The men nodded, a silent understanding without the murmur of words expressed.

By this time, everyone in the audience had shed a tear or two, and again they all observed Christopher as he made his final move to Phoebe, locking their arms and making their stroll down the red carpet.

Covered in the same shimmer of bejeweled crystals, down to four-inch heels and a sheer veil covering her face, Phoebe's heart galloped, her excitement on high boil. Being the first to become engaged, it had felt like a lifetime to get to this point, and she internally coaxed herself into putting one foot in front of the other and not sprinting to jump in Quentin's arms.

After their love session last night in the wedding suite, Phoebe thought she would be weighed down with disappointment for not staying strong and making it to the wedding like they had agreed. Instead, she felt surer than ever, her body rejoicing and her mind carrying an exuberance of needy excitement that their love session had been blessed with pure bliss. It was then that she knew abstaining from him didn't make her hungrier; instead, it gave her anxiety she never wanted to feel again. It was the revelation of all revelations, finding it unnecessary to be without him for any length of time that she thought would be appropriate.

"I've learned a valuable lesson."

Christopher paused just before the altar, turning to meet the smirk of his daughter. "I'll consider it a privilege to hear it," he said.

"Being a lawyer makes me overthink things in my personal life. While it's a good trait to have in my career, in my life, I think being more relaxed is best." She sighed. "You have been my everything, Daddy. Your teachings of showing love and being respectful, along with your relentless push to drive me to reach my goals in life have everything to do with this moment right now."

More tears clouded Christopher's gaze. "I cannot thank you enough for loving my sisters and me equally. And if you've ever felt that you weren't enough, I'm here to tell you, God makes no mistakes, He knew you would be able to bear the things we've gone through, and He was right. You're the real MVP, and no man could ever replace the love I have for you."

His face was soaked now, and he wrapped Phoebe in

his arms so tightly that their heartbeats matched as heat settled along their skin.

"I love you so much, baby," he whispered. "And I thank you for this teachable moment. Have the time of your life, and if there's anything, anything at all you ever need, you know where to find me."

They pulled away just in time to notice Quentin standing at their side, his arm carrying around them both as the three of them embraced tightly, fragrances of cologne and perfume wafting around them.

At once they pulled away, with Christopher and Quentin's hands meeting in unison for a shake.

"You have my word," was all Quentin said.

Christopher nodded, then winked down at Phoebe as she was shuffled to the altar to stand before her fiancé.

Sniffles ran throughout the venue, and Christopher took a step back but didn't sit as he waited for three bishops to ask the question that had daunted his mind.

It didn't take long for the words to be spoken,

"Dearly beloved, we are gathered here in the sight of God and man to witness the union of Quentin Davidson, Phoebe Alexandria Rose, Luke Steele, Jasmine Alexandria Rose, Derek James Clark, and Eden Alexandria Rose, in holy matrimony."

"Woooo!" an audience member called out, causing the entire congregation to light up in laughter. The trio turned with smiles to find Carla whooping with a fist-pumping in the air, then settling down as she stuck her tongue out and winked at them all.

"Who gives these three women to marry these three men?" the bishop continued without pause.

Christopher held his head high as he eyed all three daughters, then all three men, a clamor behind his chest as he responded with certainty.

"I do."

They all smiled and exhaled visibly without realizing they were holding their breaths.

"Do you Quentin Davidson, take Phoebe Alexandria Rose, to be your lawfully wedded wife, to love and honor her, keeping the promises of her heart in sickness and in health as long as you both shall live?"

The camera crews could see the radiance of Quentin's smile from the far corners of the room, and as they zoomed in to gauge his response, could feel the adoration pouring from him.

"I do," he said.

"Phoebe Alexandria Rose, do you take Quentin Davidson to be your lawfully wedded husband, to honor and love him, keeping the promises of his heart in sickness and in health as long as you both shall live?"

Phoebe's smile equally matched Quentin's.

"You're damn right I do."

The crowd chuckled, and Quentin pulled her in, their hearts dancing off one another as he attempted to skip straight to the kiss. He held her there as the bishop offered

Luke and Jasmine, and Derek and Eden the same question. After all of them said *I do,* another long whoop and clap echoed from the crowd as the bishop continued.

"Repeat after me."

One by one, they said their vows, another promise of love everlasting, for better or worse, cherishing one another for all time. Tears were now falling from each of them as they were wrapped in pure elation and extreme satisfaction of the moment.

As the ring carrier, Jonas Alexander Rose strolled with his son to all three couples, congratulating them while offering their rings.

Exchanging the sacred jewelry came with another intake of heavy breath, and each couple glanced down at their hands then back at each other, sparkles and winks in their eyes as they moved to the final part of the ceremony.

"By the virtue appointed in me, under the laws of the state of Illinois, I now pronounce you all husband and wife. You may kiss your brides."

All at once, Quentin, Luke, and Derek lifted the veils from their wives' faces, wrapping them so tightly neither could inhale without the other.

The kisses were slow, tantalizing thumping zings of expressive energy as lips meshed, and tongues explored the inner recesses of their mouths. They inhaled each other, instantly aroused by the capture of not only the kiss but the intermediate entanglement of souls that sealed them together, making them one simultaneously.

The crowd went crazy with shouts of congratulations, clapping, stomps, and cameras flashing in an illumination of excitement.

When it came time for the couples to depart, they lingered for moments embracing one another. Hand in hand, each couple turned toward their guests and held their hands up, pulling another round of screaming shouts and stomps from the crowd.

All were in attendance: the entire Rose family, the Royals of Kéra Asnela, the Clarks, the Steeles, the Davidsons, along with news reporters and camera crews from each of the main stations that recorded the live event.

The men glanced to their wives, and they all nodded, then together they left the altar, hand in hand in a sexy stroll down their respective red carpets.

Rose petals were tossed instead of rice, and as they reached the exit, they all made their way to the courtyard where the reception would be held, complete with live entertainment, dancing, and also where three award-winning chefs were waiting to take orders with a full Hell's Kitchen staff at their command.

STANDING IN THE CUT AWESTRUCK BY THE SENTIMENTAL ceremony, Carla's heart had never been so full. Witnessing the sheer happiness and love of her girlfriends made her wonder if she'd ever find that type of blissfulness of her own.

"A penny for your thoughts," a dark voice strummed.

A soft smile lifted the corners of her mouth as a spinning web of heat shot into her panties.

"Trust me, my thought's prices are on the rise. Are you sure you can afford them," she teased, spinning on her heels to face the dark brown undercut of his sharp chin.

"Give me a second to check my bank account because the way it's set up…"

Carla tossed her head back and laughed, recognizing his joke before it could be completed. Jacob chuckled.

"Somehow, I gather with all these festivities, you're ready to take the ultimate plunge."

A correlating heat swept over Carla's skin as a rigorous pulse knocked between her thighs. "With you? Maybe. You know, there's a wedding suite upstairs."

The guffaw that drummed from his lips caused her nerves to tighten and he eyed Carla so intensely her spine tingled.

Carla Jones had been pretty upfront about her interest in Jacob Alexander Rose, and he had returned that curiosity, but they'd both been keeping that attentiveness at a very low level.

"Yes, I do," he said, "but before we go there, I've got something else to show you first."

Chapter Seven

*J*acob took Carla's hand in his. "I'd like to be proper with what I want to say next, so let me ask you, Ms. Carla Jones, are you seeing anyone?"

A trail of unnoticeable chills scurried down Carla's spine.

"It depends on what you mean by seeing," she responded. "I have male friends, if that's what you're asking.

His gaze lowered. "Does your heart belong to any of these *friends*?"

"No," she answered quickly.

His crescent smile lit up the temperature of her flesh, and at the same time, Jacob was internally attempting to comprehend the sudden jealousy that had knotted in his gut.

"*Perfezionare*," he responded in the Italian tongue.

Piqued, Carla's brow rose.

"It means—"

"Perfect," she finished.

Now it was Jacob's turn to be surprised as his thick brows dipped. A sudden heat crawled over his skin at her understanding of the foreign language.

"You speak the dialect," he said, more of a recognition than a question.

"I'm a teacher, Mr. Rose. My studies include language arts and a portion of that deals with teaching foreign linguistic studies at the high school."

"Ms. Carla Jones," his deep voice drawled, "you are becoming more fascinating by the second."

Carla laughed, the melody of her mirth making his heart somersault.

"I'd like to take you out on a date. There's a restaurant on Thirty-Eight and Magnolia that I think you would enjoy."

Her heart pattered. "How would you know what I would enjoy?"

Jacob's tongue traced his lips, and Carla couldn't help but follow the slip of his wet muscle. She shivered in response. He sucked off his bottom lip with the press of his tongue and teeth.

"We seem to have a connection, yes?"

"*Sì.*"

His grin broadened. "Then humor me and know that I have an inkling of your tastes in mind."

A tactful sparkle in her eye was caught by the magnetic pull of his gaze.

"Just say when."

Jacob held his arm out, and Carla wrapped her own arms around it. He pulled her close, giving her a whiff of his Christian Clive cologne.

Assaulted by his masculinity, Carla's body hummed with delight as her soft frame grooved against the rough ridges of his hard physique.

Dressed in Armani much like the rest of the grooms-men, Jacob's entire persona was cloaked in dark chocolate skin. The red necktie, pocket square, and the peek of a black button-down shirt highlighted the tone of his melanin.

Carla remembered when Eden had referred to him as a Lance Gross look-alike, but Carla had refuted that claim. Not because their images weren't familiar—more so because as handsome as the actor was, her memory of him was that of a comedian from specific roles he'd played. Instead, Jacob carried the maturity of his thirty-eight years immaculately, his charisma laced with the age of a refined gentleman.

"How about tomorrow night?"

They strolled arm in arm, the two making their way to the courtyard.

"I'd like that." She hesitated, then asked, "Dinner?"

They paused, and Jacob eyed her, his gaze simmering as he kept a stronghold on her dark brown orbs.

"I think lunch would be preferable, as dinner would make for a larger appetite."

Carla shivered and Jacob felt her quake. "Cold?"

"Not in the least."

He smirked. "I know you came here with the brides-maids but save a dance for me, *Bellissima*."

"Hmm, you think I'm beautiful?" She questioned his compliment.

He lifted her hand to his mouth for a kiss. "I don't think. I know. Your spirit complements itself, and of course, your outer beauty is an added bonus."

They proceeded with their stroll, lingering closely as they entered the courtyard just in time to catch the end of Jonathon Alexander Rose's speech.

It wasn't ironic that their seats were beside one another since they'd been paired up in their walk down the aisle during the ceremony.

He pulled out her chair and she sat. Then he swiftly took his seat, relaxing as their attention was pulled toward the speaker.

With a wine glass in his hand, Jonathon held it high. All in attendance followed his lead.

"To my beautiful sisters and my brothers from another mother, may you have long lives and bear an abundance of children together. I've never been more proud to welcome in-laws into the family in my life."

Somebody cleared their throat, and all eyes turned to Norma Rodriguez, their father's newlywed wife.

A guffaw resounded around the room.

"That doesn't include you, Mama Rodriguez," he assured.

A tinkering of snickers ran throughout the room as others coughed in interruption, especially since the entire Rose family were newly married within the last year or so. It had been one fairy-tale romance and wedding after another, as if their destinies were aligned on a link of matrimonial bliss.

"All right, all right," Jonathon said, "I get your point."

Everyone laughed, and cameras flashed as the wedding party enjoyed their playful banter.

"Seriously," Jonathon's stern gaze went back to Quentin, Luke, and Derek, "welcome to the family."

"Here, here!"

A round of applause reverberated, and everyone took a sip of the bubbly that had been on ice most of the morning.

"And now," Jonathon kept his gaze on them, "the dance floor awaits you."

The newlyweds rose to the occasion, all three strolling to the floor for their first dance as husband and wife.

One dance turned into two, then three, before they were all interrupted, one after the other, by the grooms' fathers who wanted to get their own groove on with the brides.

When Fredrick Clark approached Derek and Eden, Derek haphazardly drew Eden closer, as if being heart to heart wasn't close enough. Besides not being ready to part from her, if only for the short length of a solitary tune, Derek wanted to protect Eden from his father's whorish spirit.

Having previously spoken his truth to Derek about never loving his mother while simultaneously offering Derek advice to wed the potential mother of his child instead of Eden because he considered it the right thing to do, Derek had almost not invited the old man. But after much consideration, and with Eden's blessing, he'd done it anyway.

"Congratulations," Fredrick said, glancing from Eden over to Derek.

"Thank you," Eden chimed, her eyes filled to the rim with longing for her husband.

Fredrick took note of the stringent way Derek held Eden close, a sigh escaping his lips. "Son, do you mind if I dance with your bride?"

Derek made sure to keep his father's eye when he responded, "As a matter of fact, I do."

"Babe."

Derek didn't make the mistake to glance down into Eden's soft loving gaze. He'd give her anything she wanted if he did, and he planned to stand by his determination.

Fredrick slipped his hands into his pockets and nodded. "I understand."

"Good."

"If you don't mind, could I at least have a word with you?"

Derek sighed. "When this song is over, you'll have the time before the next tune to say whatever is on your chest."

Eden locked her jaw and glanced away. She couldn't imagine how it must have felt for Derek to hear such a raw, uncut revelation from his father during a time they should've been celebrating the award Derek was being presented with.

"What are you doing up here instead of at your reserved seat downstairs?" Fredrick asked, placing a hand on Derek's shoulder as he held the other out for a shake.

Derek accepted his father's greeting. "Thinking."

Fredrick and Malik, Derek's brother, glanced between each other.

"It must be important if it's pulled your attention away from the honor you're here to receive tonight."

Derek cleared his throat. He wasn't in the habit of going to his father for advice when it came to relationships, especially since he grew up with Fredrick insisting they were a distraction. But with his father and brother both waiting for an answer to the thing that spelled him, Derek spoke, "I'm in love with Eden."

Both Malik and Fredrick continued to stare, the silence thick.

"I may have a child with another woman. Someone from my past." He sighed. "Instead of being honest with Eden about it, I tried to find a resolution on my own. Long story short, Eden

found out and now..." The space around them became quiet again as they listened, and Derek searched for the words. "It's coming between us."

"It will only get worse," Fredrick said.

Derek tensed, his jaw locking as he lifted his eyes to his father.

Fredrick sighed. "This is what I've been warning you about your entire life. And now, you're going to have to marry her."

Both Malik's and Derek's intense gazes lowered into a scowl.

"Marry who, exactly?"

"Your child's mother, who else?"

"You're out of your damn mind," Derek's dark voice fired. "And furthermore, I don't know if she's my child's mother yet." Derek shook his head. "This is your advice? What about Eden?"

Fredrick waved a hand. "She'll get over you eventually, and vice versa. You'll learn to love your child's mother, and all will be fair. You're a Clark. You take care of your responsibilities even if it means you suffer for it. Trust me, I know."

The room became still again as Derek's and Malik's questionable gazes turned into frowns.

"What are you saying?"

"I've been where you are, and I chose to do the honorable thing and marry my children's mother." He slipped a tongue across his teeth, then sucked. "I learned to love her. I cared for her, and I love the hell out of my kids. But I was never truly in love with your mother. I was in love with someone else."

The sting of his word had punched Derek and his brother Malik in the gut with velocity. However, Derek didn't have the time to process it all as he was being called to the stage at the National Association of Realtor's awards ceremony as a runner-up nominee.

Fredrick sighed harshly. "How about this. I won't take up too much more of you and your bride's moment. I didn't come here to fuss or be a bad taste in anyone's mouth. You do know all these years I thought I was protecting you by telling you not to get involved with—"

"Get to the point... Father."

Derek's stern terse pronunciation made Fredrick pause, then nod and backtrack. "I never meant to hurt you with my advice, however bad it was, and I'm sorry." He glanced at Eden. "My apologies to you, too, Mrs. Ros—Clark," he fumbled. Fredrick cleared his throat. "It is tradition that the father of the groom cover the expense of the honeymoon for the newlywed couple."

"That's quite all right, Father. I've got it handled."

Fredrick pressed his lips closed tightly and nodded. "I was afraid you might say that. Even if you never accept my gift, I left it on the table with all the others anyway."

"Thank you," Eden chimed while Derek only tilted his head in a single nod.

"Congratulations to you both."

"Are you leaving?" Eden asked.

"Yeah. I think I've worn out my welcome."

Fredrick nodded a farewell, then turned and strode across the dance floor, past a dozen tables, and out of the building.

Chapter Eight

"*A*re you okay?"

Derek pulled his focus back to Eden and leaned into her mouth for a kiss. "Did you feel that?"

A lustrous smile tugged at her lips. "I sure did," she purred.

"Not that," he chuckled. "I mean that rhythm between us."

"Our heartbeats?"

"Yes."

"How could I ever miss it?"

He pressed his forehead into hers. "Then you know I've never been better. Thank you so much for making me the happiest man alive."

Eden turned her lips up, and he captured her mouth.

"Mmmm..."

"I love you, Mrs. Clark."

"And I love you, Mr. Clark."

Their smiles were joined when they kissed, heat coiling them as they swayed to the music, entangled in an embrace.

Not much further away, Phoebe slipped her hands up Quentin's chest, her arms circling his thick neck.

"I've got something for you," she cooed.

A brow hiked up his brilliantly designed chocolate face.

"Oh yeah?"

"Yeah."

"Is it anything close to what you gave me last night?"

Phoebe giggled. "Nothing is better than that."

Quentin wiggled his brows. "Whatcha got for me, woman?"

Phoebe nodded over at stepmom Norma, who strolled across the floor in a black and red gown that clung to her voluptuous figure. She handed an envelope to Phoebe.

"Thank you, Momma Norma," Phoebe said.

"The pleasure's all mine. Congratulations to you both." She winked up at Quentin, and he returned the gesture just as she strolled away.

Peering down at Phoebe, Quentin split a glance between the envelope in her hand and Phoebe's mischievous leer.

"Open it."

They paused the sway of their hips, long enough for

Quentin to take his finger along the groove of the sealed packet and remove the piece of paper.

When his eyes fell across the words, his mouth lifted, dark eyes highlighting as a strumming laugh fell from his lips.

A map with different color regions covered the document, and to the left was each country, and the appropriate percentage of DNA found in the ancestry test.

Quentin immediately remembered the night they'd strolled hand in hand into the United Center, home of the Chicago Bulls and Blackhawks NHL team.

"You can always get a DNA test done to find out your ancestry."

"I've always wanted to do that."

"We should do it together."

Phoebe stopped walking and turned to him. *"We should, shouldn't we?"*

"Absolutely," Quentin's voice bolstered, holding a James Earl Jones beat. "For all I know, I could be an African prince around here." His intimidation made Phoebe giggle, and before long, she burst into laughter.

"And I an African princess." She laughed.

Quentin pulled her in for a hug. "Or a Nigerian princess," his thick voice drummed.

It made Phoebe shudder, and she pulled Quentin's face closer to hers. "Or you a Nigerian prince," she said.

Quentin leaned even closer, with his mouth hovering right above hers.

"Or you an Indian princess," he continued.

When his mouth sank into hers, Phoebe purred, "Or you an Indian prince..."

Coming out of his reverie, Quentin's gaze sparkled over at Phoebe.

"Thirty-eight percent Nigerian..." he drawled.

Phoebe bit her bottom lip, her checks stretched with heat on a blush.

"Now I have to have my ancestry completed."

"I was hoping you might say that."

"Yeah?"

"I've got a kit for you."

Quentin's burly guffaw made butterflies spiral in Phoebe's stomach.

"You're so handsome when you laugh."

He drew her back close. "Only when I laugh?"

She slapped at his arm. "No, silly."

"I'm just kidding. Thank you. It is your spirit that brings me joy. There is no other alive more elated than I am in this moment, right now."

Phoebe blushed and leaned into his lips where their kiss sent off a detonation of bursting heat.

"I say we find a quiet corner. No one will miss us, don't you think?"

Her giggled turned into a heavy laugh, and she shook her head. "I think they might notice, babe; after all, we're only the highlight of this shindig."

He met her exuberant laugh with a kiss, their forever

sealed off in not only the tango of their tongues but the thread from one heartbeat to another.

THE SPIRIT OF THE WEDDING PARTY WAS BURSTING WITH upbeat festivity as couples danced, sipped from champagne flutes, and laughed with boisterous energy. Across the eloquently designed room, at a long rectangular table covered in the silver and white theme cloth with rose petals creating a red runner appearance down the center were the Royals of Kéra Asnela.

At the head of the table, King Isaac Winthrope rose from his seat, his royal guard moving as he did. They paused as he held up a hand to halt his security, then he proceeded across the floor where he approached the groom's family table.

"Excuse me, madame."

Turning her light brown eyes up to meet his russet gaze, Cynthia Denise Clark smiled, a query flashing across her face as she responded, "Your Royal Highness, how can I be of assistance to you?"

The king struck her with his penetrating gaze, the beat of his heart banging against his chest as he took in Cynthia's natural frosty shoulder-length curls. He'd felt an uncanny energy spiraling from her from the moment she'd presented herself on the arm of her son, Malik Anthony Clark.

They'd entered Architectural Artifacts and found their seating promptly. She appeared graceful, elegantly wrapped in an American designer gown, with her arms on display, the most striking deep chocolate brown he'd ever seen.

"I'd like to introduce myself appropriately. I'm Isaac Winthrope. Some people address me as king. It might have something to do with a tribe I rule back across seas."

Cynthia chuckled at his teasing while at the same time wondering if he was really this down-to-earth royal or if he was secretly just as pompous as most imperial families. Still, the dialect in which his words were wielded hit her skin with an outpouring of warmth, something she hadn't felt in years.

"I'm aware of who you are, King Isaac Winthrope," she bashfully responded. "I'm Cynthia De—"

"Denise Clark, mother and queen of the Clarks of Northshire Bend."

Cynthia's brow rose. "Well, I don't know about a queen, but yes."

"No?" King Winthrope tsked. "Now you know." He paused as they eyed each other, then he held out a hand. "Is it possible for me to lead you in a waltz?"

Her hand slipped across his burly palm. "I would like that."

King Isaac Winthrope helped her to her feet, taking a respectful step back as she slipped into the comfort of his shadow.

"This way," he said, arm out as Cynthia nodded and eased in front of him, her mature hips suddenly taking a life of their own as they sashayed with confidence to the dance floor.

There, everyone in the area grooved to the tempo that surrounded them, indulging in the potency of love that showered the courtyard of guests.

Note from the Author

HEY, READING FAMILY! I HOPE YOU ENJOYED THIS WEDDING novella and the last look we'll get up close and personal with Phoebe, Eden, and Jasmine. (Insert tears here) It's so surreal to say that, but the truth is the Falling for a Rose series is nearing its end.

Even though I know this, actually playing out this idea is making me sweat. I love this family. We've grown together, and I've had the pleasure of watching them fall in love. We've seen their hurts, pains, their fallouts, and more, so it's so hard to say goodbye.

Before you ask, yes, Jacob and Carla get their own story, and it is the very last of the main Rose family romances. With that said, I am playing with the idea of writing novella/short stories with holiday updates on what's going on with the family. So they are not entirely gone but just living their best lives and giving us a piece of it every once in a while.

Some of you may be asking, what about those cousins. Ya know, Antonio Rose's sons. They're Roses, too, right?

Correct! And I have also played around with the idea of bringing their stories to life as well. As a matter of fact, there's a full family tree that you can browse through and discover who's connected to who and other information complete with ages, birthdays, spouses, children, occupations, and more! Check out the link below.

Also, if you'd like to connect with me, the place to be is my Facebook group. There's a book discussion two weeks after every release, and I'd love to have you!

Here's what you don't want to miss! Get a free teaser on Jonas and Samiyah, a never-published, never-before-seen short story when you subscribe to my newsletter!

And oh...if you enjoyed *Promising Forever*, leave me a

review and tell me about it! I'd love to hear from you, and doing so means a lot to me.

XOXO – Stephanie

Connect with Me on Instagram!
The Rose Family Tree

93

Contemporary Romance

- Everything I Always Wanted (A Friends to Lovers Romance)
- Safe with Me (Falling for a Rose Book One)
- Enough (Falling for a Rose Book Two)
- Only If You Dare (Falling for a Rose Book Three)
- Fever (Falling for a Rose Book Four)
- A Lifetime with You (Falling for a Rose Book Five)
- She said Yes (Falling for a Rose Holiday Edition Book Six)
- Mine (Falling for a Rose Book Seven)
- The Sweetest Surrender (Falling for a Rose Book Eight)
- Tempted By You (Falling for a Rose Book Nine)
- No Holds Barred (In the Heart of a Valentine Book One)
- A Risqué Engagement (In the Heart of a Valentine Book Two)
- Give Me A Reason (In the Heart of a Valentine Book Three)

- A Game-Changing Christmas (A Falling for a Rose & In the Heart of A Valentine, Holiday Edition)
- If I Could Stay (Lunch Break Series Book One)
- With Your Permission (In The Heart of A Valentine Book Five)
- Wait No More (A With Your Permission Spin-Off)
- On The Naughty List (Prelude to Her Naughty Suitor)
- Her Naughty Suitor (Falling for a Rose Book Ten)

Romantic Suspense Thrillers

- Beautiful Assassin
- Beautiful Assassin 2 Revelations
- Mistaken Identity

Crime Fiction

- Prowl
- Prowl 2
- Hidden

Fantasy

- Golden (Rapunzel's F'd Up Fairytale)

Non-Fiction

- Against All Odds (Surviving the Neonatal Intensive Care Unit) *Non-Fiction

About the Author

Stephanie Nicole Norris is an author from Chattanooga, Tennessee, with a humble beginning. She was raised with six siblings by her mother Jessica Ward. Always being a lover of reading, during Stephanie's teenage years, her joy was running to the bookmobile to read stories by R. L. Stine.

After becoming a young adult, her love for romance sparked, leaving her captivated by heroes and heroines alike. With a big imagination and a creative heart, Stephanie penned her first novel *Trouble in Paradise* and self-published it in 2012. Her debut novel turned into a four-book series packed with romance, drama, and suspense. As a prolific writer, Stephanie's catalog continues to grow. Her books can be found on her website and Amazon. Stephanie is inspired by the likes of Donna Hill, Eric Jerome Dickey, Jackie Collins, and more. She currently resides in Tennessee with her husband and four-year-old son.

https://stephanienicolenorris.com/

Made in the USA
Columbia, SC
13 May 2020